# CASEY JONES
## AND HIS RAILROAD LEGACY

Retold by
**CHRISTOPHER ALBER**

Illustrated by
**RICHARD MADISON**

Cavendish Square
New York

3 4028 08493 5544
HARRIS COUNTY PUBLIC LIBRARY

WITHDRAWN

J B Jones
Alber, Christopher
Casey Jones and his
railroad legacy
$10.58
ocn856902899
First edition.    06/25/2014

On a bright spring morning in 1863, in a small southeastern Missouri town, Frank Jones, a local schoolteacher, and his wife Anne welcomed their baby boy John.

Life in rural America was very simple in those days. People from rural areas did not get a chance to make money or a name for themselves.

2

One day, Frank got a job offer from a well-known school in Kentucky. He was very excited. "My children will have a better chance and a better life in Kentucky. We should move there as soon as we can," he thought. So they packed their bags and headed for Kentucky.

John was only thirteen. He had never traveled by train before. While they were waiting at the station, he saw a train for the first time. CHUG, CHUG, CHUG. A huge engine pulled into the station.

There were huge puffs of gray smoke coming out of the smokestack of the train – just like clouds. WOOT-WOOT! WOOT-WOOT! The train whistle blew to warn people standing on the platform of its arrival.

John got into the train with the rest of his family. He sat next to the window and watched the trees whiz past. He watched the train chug on over running rivers, through green fields, thick forests, tall mountains, and deep valleys. He was captivated.

After eight long hours in the train, they finally reached the lush green fields of Cayce, Kentucky.

John made up his mind that day. He knew exactly what he wanted to do for the rest of his life. He wanted to become an engine driver. He had found his calling.

When he was just fifteen, John began working for Mobile & Ohio Railroad as a telegrapher. Telegraphers worked with railroad companies. Back then, telegraphs were as important as e-mails are today.

John was happy working as a telegrapher but continued to dream of becoming an engine driver. Every time he heard of a job opening on the main rail line, he would request to be transferred.

A few months passed, and John's boss told him about a job for a breakman. Finally, John could get his chance! There was only one problem—John would have to move to Tennessee, where he didn't know anyone, for this new job.

But John didn't mind moving to a new state. He convinced his parents to let him go, and he set off on a new adventure.

John was tall and strong. This is why he was well suited for work on the railroad. He had to tough it out sometimes, often carrying heavy loads for very long distances. John moved up the ranks very fast. Soon, he was the fireman on the train.

He was also a friendly, good-natured man. This made all his coworkers like him very much. After a long, hard day at work, they liked to go out and relax in the evenings.

One of the most frequently visited boarding houses in the area belonged to a Mrs. Brady. The boys often went there after their shift to enjoy the fresh air and pleasant conversation.

John was invited there one day. Mrs. Brady was particular about the kind of people who visited, so newcomers were subjected to questioning.

"Who is this young lad?"
asked Mrs. Brady.

"He is the new fireman,"
said one of the men.

"Where are you from?"
asked Mrs. Brady.

"Cayce, Kentucky," he replied.

"Sit down then, Casey," she announced.

From then on, he was called Casey Jones.

Janie, Mrs. Brady's daughter, helped with the work.

"Janie!" shouted Mrs. Brady. "Where are you? Come out here and help me serve coffee to these young men."

Janie's brown hair was long and thick. She had eyes as bright as diamonds and lips as red as a rose.

Casey looked at her delicate hands pouring the coffee. He felt himself falling in love with her instantly.

Janie too felt drawn towards this handsome young man. He courted her, and in a few years they were married.

The happy couple bought a home in the city and began raising a family. They had three children and were very happy.

Casey continued to do well at his job, and soon enough, he earned his dream of becoming an engine driver. Casey worked with Sim Webb, who was his fireman. They soon earned a reputation for being the railroad's best team.

Casey was very proud of his job. He was proud of the fact that his train was never late. No matter how hard he had to work, or how fast he had to drive, his train was known for being on time. In fact, it is said that Casey was so punctual that people would set their watches to his train!

Another one of Casey's unique talents was the way he would blow the train whistle. He would make a long, drawn-out note that began softly, rose, and died away to a whisper. Everyone knew that it was Casey in the engine when they heard that sound. They called it the whippoorwill whistle.

"There's Casey Jones," people would say, as he whizzed past their towns.

One day, Casey and Sim had just finished their shift and were gathering their things to go home. Just as they were about to leave, they were told that another driver, Joe Lewis, had fallen ill and would not be able to drive his train that night.

"Will you be able to take his place?" their boss asked them.

"Of course we will," said both men in unison. Casey was never known to turn down a task, even if it meant working longer than necessary.

"The train is a little late," said the supervisor. "But don't worry; I have given you a clear track. All other trains and engines have been told to move to side tracks so that you can speed straight into Canton."

The weather had been rainy and foggy. There were dark clouds looming. Many men might have canceled their journey, but Casey was confident. He knew he was the best engine driver there was. If he couldn't do it, no one could.

Casey began building up speed. WHOOSH! He was going so fast, that before you saw the train, it was gone. Casey was making good time. He was quite sure he would reach his destination on time—as always.

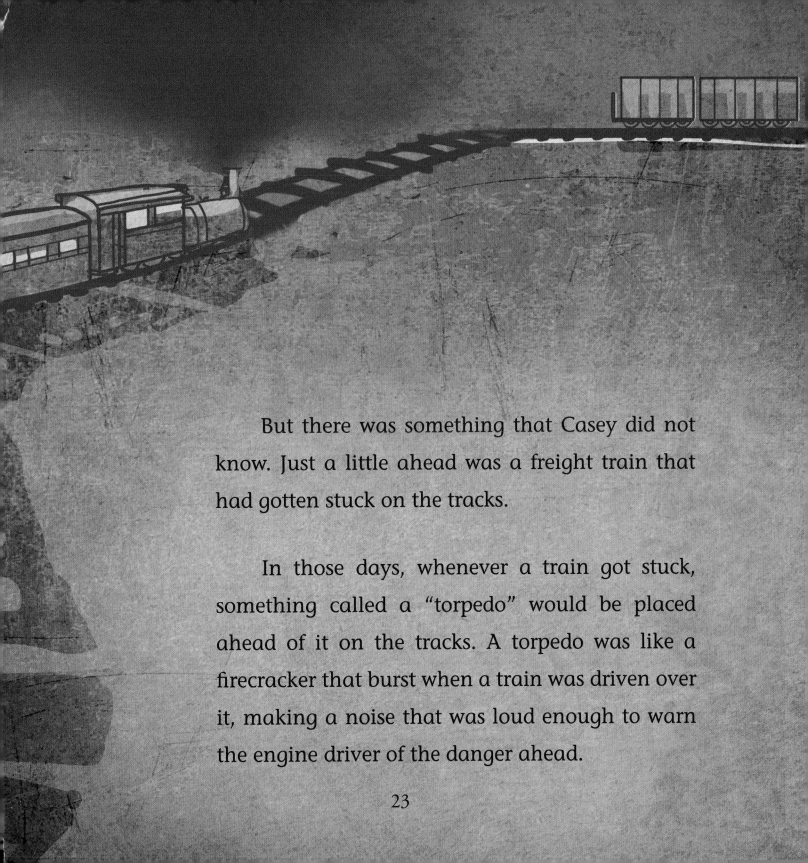

But there was something that Casey did not know. Just a little ahead was a freight train that had gotten stuck on the tracks.

In those days, whenever a train got stuck, something called a "torpedo" would be placed ahead of it on the tracks. A torpedo was like a firecracker that burst when a train was driven over it, making a noise that was loud enough to warn the engine driver of the danger ahead.

Because of the rain and fog, Casey had not seen the freight train. He hit the torpedo. It burst with a loud BOOM!

"Watch out!" yelled Sim. "We're going to hit something."

Both men knew that there was no way to stop the train completely. Casey stood up and pulled on the air-brake lever as hard as he could.

"Jump, Sim! Jump!" he yelled. "Save yourself."

Sim jumped. The wheels of the train began screeching as Casey tried to get the train to stop. He could see the train now. It was too close. There was no way to avoid the accident. He pulled hard on the train's shrill whistle to warn anyone in the way to get out.

For Casey, it seemed like an eternity. But within seconds, his engine, No. 382, crashed into the back of the stalled freight train.

Hearing the collision, people came to help. They found all the passengers safe and sound. Unfortunately, Casey Jones' body was found in the ruins of the engine. One hand was on the whistle, and the other on the air-brake lever. He had died doing what he loved best.

But the legend does not end here. Wallace Sanders, who had worked as Casey's engine wiper, deeply mourned the death of his dear friend. In Casey's memory, Wallace wrote a song that he would hum while cleaning engines.

The song was very catchy, and it slowly spread. Everyone started to sing the song. Soon, it became a leading folksong and was eventually published. Casey Jones became a legend. Today, over a hundred years later, some people still sing the beautiful ballad of Casey Jones.

# ABOUT CASEY JONES

The story of Casey Jones is a true one. He was a brave engine driver who took great pride in his work. He could have saved his life by jumping out of the train with Sim, but didn't because he knew that if he did not keep the air-brake lever pulled for as long as possible, there would be a greater chance of his passengers dying.

The era during which this took place was very different from today. Trains were a lot more susceptible to accidents and Casey Jones wasn't the only man to die in a train wreck. However, Casey has been immortalized in Wallace's song, and that is why we still remember him today.

# WORDS TO KNOW

*Brakeman:* The brakeman was the man whose job was to assist in stopping the train by applying brakes in each individual wagon.

*Fireman:* In steam engines, there were always two men required in the engine. One would navigate the train while the other would just put the coal in the furnace. The man who supplied the fuel was called the fireman.

*Freight Train:* Trains that transport cargo and other goods are called freight trains. These are different from passenger trains.

*Punctual:* Being punctual means being on time.

*Telegraph:* The telegraph was a system by which messages could be transferred over long distances electronically. Though it is very outdated now, it was a great discovery at that time.

# TO FIND OUT MORE

**BOOKS:**

Brimner, Larry D. *Casey Jones*. Minneapolis: Compass Point Books (2004).

Drummond, Allan. *Casey Jones*. New York: Farrar, Straus and Giroux (BYR) (2001).

Garland, Michael. *Casey Jones*. Mankato: Child's World Inc (2012).

**WEBSITES:**

http://www.watervalley.net/users/caseyjones/mrs~cj.htm

You can read an interview that Janie Jones gave in a magazine about her husband and the incident when she was still alive.

http://www.biography.com/people/casey-jones-9357038

You can hear the famous song about Casey in this link. You can also play fascinating "train games" here.

http://americanfolklore.net/folklore/2010/07/casey_jones.html

Read the 1928 article in the *Erie Railroad Magazine*, an interview with Janie Jones, published twenty-eight years after Casey's death.

Harris County Public Library
Houston, Texas

Published in 2014 by Cavendish Square Publishing, LLC
303 Park Avenue South, Suite 1247, New York, NY 10010
Copyright © 2014 by Cavendish Square Publishing, LLC
First Edition

No part of this publication may be reproduced, stored in a retrieval system, or transmitted in any form or by any
means—electronic, mechanical, photocopying, recording, or otherwise—without the prior permission of the copyright
owner. Request for permission should be addressed to Permissions, Cavendish Square Publishing, 303 Park Avenue
South, Suite 1247, New York, NY 10010. Tel (877) 980-4450; Fax (877) 980-4454.

Website: cavendishsq.com
This publication represents the opinions and views of the author based on his or her personal experience,
knowledge, and research. The information in this book serves as a general guide only. The author and publisher
have used their best efforts in preparing this book and disclaim liability rising directly or indirectly from the use and
application of this book.
CPSIA Compliance Information: Batch #WW14CSQ
All websites were available and accurate when this book was sent to press.
LIBRARY OF CONGRESS CATALOGING-IN-PUBLICATION DATA
Alber, Christopher.
Casey Jones/Christopher Alber.
pages cm — (American legends and folktales)
Includes bibliographical references.
ISBN 978-1-62712-283-2 (hardcover) ISBN 978-1-62712-284-9 (paperback) ISBN 978-1-62712-285-6 (ebook)
1. Jones, Casey, 1863-1900—Juvenile literature. 2. Locomotive engineers—United States—Biography—Juvenile
literature. [1. Jones, Casey, 1863-1900. 2. Locomotive engineers.]
I. Title.
TJ603.5.J66A64 2014
385.3'6092—dc23

Printed in the United States of America

Editorial Director: Dean Miller
Art Director: Jeffrey Talbot

Content and Design by quadrum
www.quadrumltd.com